To Josh
Always Remember
Rule 1 - Have FUN!

The Amazing
Alexander
The First Set

Written by Justin S. Meitz

Illustrations: Matthew C. Jones
Creative Editor: Thomas W. Cantrell

The Amazing Alexander: The First Set
Copyright ©2008 by Justin Meitz

ISBN: 978-0-615-21888-5
$17.95

Printed in China
First Printing, First Edition

The Team
Author: Justin S. Meitz
Illustrator: Matthew C. Jones
Creative Editor: Thomas W. Cantrell
Designer: Eric Barkle

www.TheAmazingAlexander.com
www.MatthewJonesDesign.org
www.TomCantrell.com
www.M2Results.com

Magic House Publishing

Reno, Nevada

"Alex! Get up! Get up! Get up! Grandma and Grandpa are coming over— and you have chores that need doing."

"Aw, Mom-m-m-m—five more minutes, please!" Alex yawned and fell back onto his bed with the pillow covering his face.

"Now, Alex! Now!"

"Yes, Ma'am."

His mom turned and left the room as Alex threw his bed covers into a ball at the end of the bed and stumbled toward the bathroom.

"And don't forget to lay your covers back over your bed," his mother said, walking down the stairs.

Alex stopped in his tracks. "How does she do that!" He muttered to himself.

He spread the covers back over the bed and stumbled into the bathroom.

HOW DOES SHE DO THAT!

Sitting on the sink were two one dollar bills. He picked them up, showed both sides to his sleepy reflection in the mirror, and began to fold them. One fold, two folds; and then, with a magical gesture, the two bills were transformed into a million dollar bill!

Alex smiled at his imaginary, yet amazed, audience. He showed both sides of the million dollar bill and then turned it back into two separate one dollar bills. Grandpa taught him this trick and he practiced in front of the mirror every chance he got.

"Alex, put down your tricks and brush your teeth," Alex's mother called as she poured thick yellow pancake batter into butter sizzling on the grill.

"How does she do that?" Alex was certain his mom could see things no one else could see. She knew what he was doing all the time. In thirty seconds he washed his face without soap, brushed his teeth without toothpaste, ran his fingers hastily through his matted hair, grabbed his magic money and headed downstairs to feed his cat, Merlin.

"And make sure to feed your poor cat." He looked at Merlin perched on top of his cat tree shelf looking expectantly back at him. It didn't seem like Merlin was poor. He even had a shiny green collar that matched his intense green eyes.

"Yeah, Mom, I'm on it." The bowl rattled as he filled it with dry cat food. Merlin leaped off his perch and dashed over meowing as though he hadn't eaten for years.

"Grandpa is taking you out tonight, so put on one of your nice button down shirts that Grandma gave you for Christmas," his mother insisted.

Grandma was always giving Alex un-cool striped button down shirts and itchy wool sweaters.

"Where are we going tonight?" Alex asked innocently, already knowing the answer.

"You will just have to wait and see," his mother replied mysteriously.

MERL

Alex already knew where they were going. He could hardly wait for six o'clock. He had always loved magic and tonight was the first time he would get to see a professional magic show.

His interest in magic had something to do with his grandfather always coming over and performing magic tricks for him. Recently, Alex had written a school paper about the great Harry Houdini.

MEGAN GIVES HEARING BACK TO CHILDREN IN AFRICA

MATTGIC WINS GOLD IN HALF PIPE COMPETITION

NEWS AROUND THE WORLD

FRANK WEARS SULU IN FIJI!

ASTHMA CURED BY ZOE AND JEREMY!!

BILLDINI PERFORMS CHINESE WATER TORTURE CELL IN FRONT OF MILLIONS?!!

SSSHHH!

He was fascinated at how Houdini had worked so many years to perfect his great escapes—sliding out of handcuffs, worming his way out of straitjackets, and disappearing from prison cells. But now Alex could do more than just read about it; he would see a professional magician perform magic live on stage. Alex secretly hoped he would be chosen from the audience to be included in one of the illusions.

Before they left for the show, Alex's grandfather worked with him on the Million Dollar Bill Trick.

He stood Alex in front of the full length mirror in the hallway and showed him how to hold his hand a certain way so his spectators wouldn't see anything suspicious. Alex was having difficulties turning the bill smoothly and blamed his troubles on his small hands.

"Don't worry Alex, you're doing great. Magic takes time and practice," Grandpa said smiling. "Just remember, the actual mechanics of the trick are only ten percent of the illusion. Performance and showmanship make up the rest."

"You mean like showing off?"

No, it's more like…

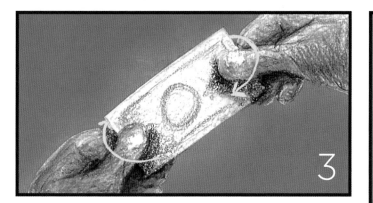

3

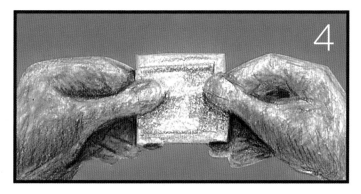

4

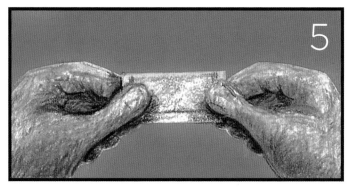

5

6

…well, here, let's try it. Take the two one dollar bills and hold them so George Washington is facing your audience—that's step two. Step three is the "show". That's when you take the bills and pretend to "show" it—you turn them around and make people think they see both sides.

Step four is to fold the bills to the right. Be sure and take your time with this step. You don't want to rush it and have the bills uneven. You want both bills to sit right behind each other with their boarders lining up perfectly.

Step five is where the magic happens. You fold the two dollar bills down and rotate the million dollar bill so it will come into view when it is unfolded.

As you do this step, bring the bills close to your face and blow on them. This distracts your audience and they won't likely notice what you are doing to the bills while you perform the secret move. This is called misdirection. Misdirection is strengthened if you look at your audience while performing the illusion, rather than looking at the bills in your hands.

Step six is unfolding the money and showing them your million dollar bill. You then do the "show" again then repeat the steps—thereby again reversing the bills. Make sure, at the end, you again show them the bills (the "show").

"Okay. I'll keep working on it in front of the mirror whenever I have time," Alex told his grandfather.

"Good boy! That will make you a good magician." Grandpa said, then paused for effect, "Do you want to know how to become a *great* magician? Make time. Make it important to practice. Do it every day— okay, six days a week. That will give you one day to goof off and give yourself a rest.

Step 2

It was time to leave for the show.

"Bye, Mom! Bye, Grandma."

"That's a lovely shirt, Alex," said his grandmother.

"Thanks Grandma," Alex smiled covertly at his mother and scratched his neck for effect.

He picked up Merlin and gave him a squeeze.

"Hissssss!" Merlin jumped down and ran off.

"Maybe someday I will make you disappear—like the tiger on TV!" Alex said teasingly as he and his grandfather walked out the door.

Alex was ready to be amazed.

MAGIC SHOW!

WITH SPECIAL GUESTS

THE MAGIC MORGAN
COLE THE MAGIC MAN
CHANDLER THE MYSTERIOUS

1813

WELCOME TO THE MOST AMAZING
MAGICAL SHOW ON EARTH!

"Grandpa where is the theater?"

"This is a very special theater, Alex. Do you see that
small booth over there?" Alex's grandfather pointed
to a stone archway with an ornate iron gate opening
to a flight of concrete steps that lead underground.
It looked like a subway entrance. "The theater is
completely underground."

There was a sign just inside the entrance. "Welcome
to the Most Amazing Magical Show on Earth!"
Grandpa smiled mysteriously as they walked down
two sets of stairs into a dimly lit foyer.

Old canvas posters of famous magicians hung on the walls. A handcuffed Houdini smiled down at Alex as if to tell him to watch the great magician escape from his restraints.

He nudged his grandfather and pointed out the cool old props scattered about the room. An antique metal banded trunk sat near a tall mirror. The edge of the mirror was pulled slightly away from the wall, like a door slightly ajar. From the opening emanated a soft light interrupted occasionally by shadows moving about like phantoms in the space behind the mirror. Suddenly two yellowish eyes peered through the opening. Alex froze, startled, and the hidden door suddenly slammed shut.

"Grandpa… did you see that?"

"See what, Alex?"

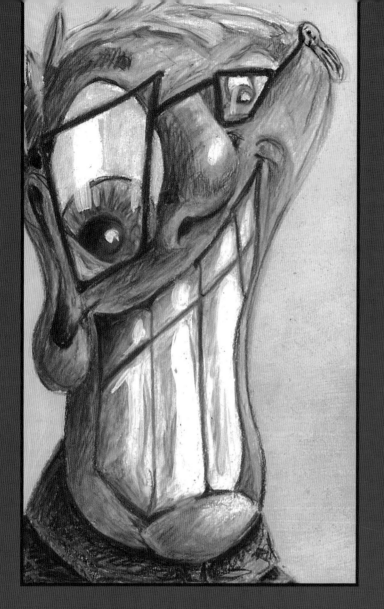

Alex looked back at the door and realized that it didn't even look like there was a door at all, just a large framed mirror that stretched from the ceiling to the floor.

"But where did…?" Alex didn't know what he just saw.

"See? It's a funny mirror. Don't I look ten feet tall and as thin as a pole?" Grandpa said and chuckled. But Alex just stood there wondering what had just happened.

"You okay, Alex?"

"Um…yeah…"

"Okay, then, let's go find our seats; it's time for the show to start."

They approached a doorway where a man pulled back the drapery revealing the entrance, and smiled mysteriously. "Enjoy the show," he said, "but beware of Medusa's snakes and Great Jericho, the magical white tiger."

Alex stayed close to his grandfather as they made their way to their seats in the front row. For some reason, Alex was not quite as excited about the possibility of being part of an illusion on stage. Maybe it was the darkened theater or the swirling lights that danced on the stage floor—or the shadows of people walking about behind the drawn curtain—or perhaps it was the memory of those strange yellow eyes staring at him from behind the crack in the door that really wasn't there.

"Alex, are you okay?"

"Um… yeah, I'm fine." Alex looked up at his grandfather. "I think I need to use the bathroom."

"The show is about to start; can't it wait?"

"Ah… yeah…" Suddenly the lights
faded to black and a single blue
spotlight focused on the stage. A man
dressed in black was standing in the light and
those same mysterious yellow eyes that Alex saw
behind the door were staring—right at him.

"No, it can't wait!" Alex muttered.
He immediately got up and went out to the foyer.

"Okay… that was spooky! Why was he staring at me with those weird eyes?" Alex was talking to himself and breathing hard. He walked past the posters that he had seen earlier. As he moved towards the bathroom, he caught sight of the strange mirror. It was slightly ajar again. This time, white fog was escaping into the hallway.

Alex felt drawn toward the mirror/door. He had to see what was behind it. He slowly opened it and cautiously stepped through. He paused for a moment, then walked slowly down a dimly lit hallway that angled to the right at the end.

His feet felt cold. He looked down and saw thick white fog covering his shoes. He felt like he was floating as he proceeded down the hallway.

"What is going on?" he wondered anxiously. He was still freaked out by the memory of those yellow eyes that were staring at him earlier. He came to the end of the hallway and turned to the right as if pulled by an invisible steel thread. He saw a black box on the floor from which poured a steady stream of billowing fog.

"Well, he thought, that's not so scary. I guess when you know how something is done, it removes the mystery." He looked around and saw an amazing array of magic props. Thick white cotton ropes and shiny steel chains were scattered throughout the room. A crystal clear triangle shaped box with knives sticking in it sat next to a large cage that held a dozen pure white doves cooing softly as they strutted about with bobbing heads. An attached cage held three sinister black ravens—with yellow eyes. In the left corner of the room was a water-filled chamber shaped like a glass casket standing on end in which were swimming what looked like several long black eels.

"That must be what the man meant by Medusa's snakes." Excitement replaced fear. "This is the coolest place ever," Alex thought. Suddenly he heard a low rumbling sound that seemed to come somewhere within the room. Fear quickly replaced excitement.

There was a large box draped with black velvet in the back of the room. Alex hadn't noticed it at first, as the black velvet blended in with the black wall behind it—which apparently it was intended to.

"Hel… um, hello?" Alex stuttered. "Is someone in there?"

There was no response. "Hello…" Alex cautiously approached the box—and there was another noise. It was a scratching sound as if someone or something was trying to escape—maybe to devour nosey ten year olds! Alex carefully circled the box but didn't move closer to it. There was no one else in the room except whomever or whatever was in the black draped object. He paused for a second then, mustering all the courage he could, he approached the box. There was no longer any noise coming from it.

"I must have imagined the sound. It's just magic equipment, nothing to be afraid of. I'll just lift the cloth off the corner and see what's inside," he told himself.

He took hold of the corner of the sheet and slowly raised it off the right side of the box.

"Rooooaaarrrr!" Hot breath hit Alex full in the face. Cold blue eyes stared unflinching at him through steel bars. The largest white tiger anyone has ever seen was standing in a steel barred cage, staring him right in the face.

Alex stifled a yell as he fell backward. This was no Merlin kitty! He scrambled to his feet and ran from the cage looking back over his shoulder as he ran—full into a heavy curtain that stood between him and safety. Panicked, he fumbled with the curtain until he found a split in the heavy velvet material and stumbled through it - and then another, and then….

…a bright white light was shining in his face.

This was not just any light, it was a spot light—and he was on stage looking in the faces of a hundred startled people. He saw his grandfather looking at him with a shocked expression on his face. Out of the corner of his eye, he saw the man in black staring at him with those strange yellow eyes. He realized that the man was the magician.

"Oh boy, what now?" he thought. As the magician continued his patter, a woman came over to Alex and whispered in his ear "Alex, my name is Megan. Don't be nervous. Just look at the audience and smile. Follow our lead and you will do great."

"Do great? What does she mean 'do great'—and how does she know my name?" He wanted to ask her, but she was already walking away and he was too nervous to say anything. He could feel his heart beating faster and faster but he managed to crack a smile at the audience.

"I'm here," he thought. "Might as well go along for the ride. Maybe Grandpa will think I was supposed to do this."

"Ladies and Gentlemen, our first volunteer for the night—Alex—Alex the Great!" The magician spoke loudly as he gestured grandly in Alex's direction. The audience clapped and Alex stood velcroed to the floor. "All I wanted to do was to go to the bathroom."

"This illusion has never before been performed with a child, but tonight we will make history. Especially if Alex survives!"

With a flourish, the magician pulled a black drape off of a small wooden table.

"As you can see, there is nothing underneath the table and nothing above. Alex, would you please come stand in front of the table?" Megan moved gracefully across the stage, gave Alex a wink and took him by his hand. She led him to the front of the table and then did a graceful twirl as she moved to the other side of the stage.

"Alex, if you would please sir, hop up here on the table and lie on your back." The magician patted the top of the table.

Now getting into the spirit of the occasion, Alex hopped up on the table, smiled at his Grandfather and leaned back into the magician's hand as he was gently lowered to the table. "This is actually fun," he thought.

"As you can see, we have two long boxes that will fit over Alex's body." The magician placed a bottomless wooden box—that was open at the upper end—over Alex's lower body. He took another that looked the same, but was open at the lower end and had a small half-moon shaped cutout that loosely fit his neck, and placed this carefully over Alex's upper body.

Alex twisted his head and looked out over the audience until he spotted his grandfather. The magician continued his patter—talking to the audience in mysterious tones. Alex's Grandfather gave him a reassuring smile and a nod.

"Ladies and Gentlemen, I warn you not to ever do this at home!"

Alex looked back at the magician. The blade was large and from Alex's view looked awfully sharp. "What are we not trying at home? I thought magic was supposed to be fun," Alex thought nervously.

"Are you ready, Alex?" The magician asked smiling down at him.

"Umm…Ready for wha…ahhh!" The magician brought down the blade between the two boxes and all the way through Alex's body. Alex didn't feel anything but he heard everyone in the audience gasp. The magician quickly produced a second blade and shoved it—apparently with some effort—down alongside the first blade. The magician reached in front of the table, unbuckled a latch and split the table in two pulling the top and bottom halves apart. The audience clapped loudly and Alex smiled in relief.

"This is so cool," Alex said out loud.

"This illusion took me a long time to perfect, said the Magician to the audience. I used to practice at home—on my two half-sisters!"

The audience laughed as the magician brought the two pieces—and Alex—back together. He withdrew the blades from between the two boxes, pretended to wipe blood off of them, and handed them to Megan. He then lifted the two boxes off the table uncovering Alex who remained whole and unharmed. Megan twirled over to the table.

"Fantastic, Alex! Hop off the table and take a bow!" Meagan skipped over to the other side of the stage and gestured back at Alex as though he was a celebrity. He sat up and jumped off the table. He looked out at the audience thinking, "This really is a lot of fun."

"Let's give Alex the Great a round of applause," The magician cried. Alex took a bow and felt like he was famous, even though he hadn't done anything but avoid getting cut in half. He hopped off the stage and plopped into his seat next to his grandfather.

"That was pretty amazing, Alex. I thought you were going to miss the show—then there you were *in* the show. How did you manage that?" Alex just grinned, thinking about his earlier backstage adventure.

The show continued. The magician survived being hung upside down in shackles in Medusa's water chamber. Megan, the magician's assistant, was transformed into a white tiger with cold blue eyes. (Alex recognized it as the same white tiger that he ran into earlier.) Magic doves and black ravens appeared from the magician's black and white gloved hands. The magician turned into Megan and Megan became the magician in an illusion called "Metamorphosis." There were flying silks, floating tables, and cards appearing out of nowhere. When the show ended, the two received a standing ovation— with enthusiastic applause and loud whistles bouncing off the vaulted ceiling.

Soon the lobby was empty except for Alex and his grandfather—and old magicians staring down at them from dusty wooden frames.

"What are we waiting for, Grandpa?"

"I think he is waiting for me." The funny mirror door opened and the magician came out of the secret hallway where Alex had entered earlier that night. "You did a very good job up there tonight, Alex, both of you!"

"Both of us?" Alex asked quizzically.

"Yes, your upper and lower half." The magician laughed and shook Alex's grandfather's hand. "Hello Phil, how have you been?"

"Aha!" Alex said "That's how Megan knew my name. You guys know each other."

"Yes, your grandfather and I are old friends. We started performing magic together in our grade school talent shows. He told me you'd be coming tonight, so I thought I would give you a real magical experience. You made it even better by choosing to follow your curiosity." He paused, then added, "It is important though, son, to respect the privacy of the magician's space—that also includes poking around in his secrets."

Alex began to stammer an apology, but the magician interrupted gently, "It's okay. It is also important for a magician to be curious; that is how we discover new magic." He continued, "My name is Thomas, Thomas Cantrell but most people know me as Raven. I created a "Black Glove to Black Raven" illusion as in the "Glove to Dove" illusion."

"Yeah, that was a cool trick, responded Alex, relieved that the magician wasn't upset with him. "Wish I could do that. It sure would freak out my cat!" The three of them laughed.

"Your grandfather said you are very interested in magic. Do you know any good magic that you could show me?" Raven asked.

"Well, Grandpa taught me how to turn two one dollar bills into a million dollar bill." Alex pulled out the two bills, turned them casually this way and that and Raven and his Grandfather applauded delightfully when it transformed into a million dollar bill.

"Well done—very well done, Alex! That's a lot of money you have there! Now I have something for you." Raven walked over to a large wooden trunk with metal bands that was sitting near a poster of Harry Houdini. He fumbled with his keys for a moment until he found a curiously shaped tarnished brass key. He opened the old trunk and pulled out a small carved wooden box with leather hinges.

"Your grandfather and I went to our first magic show when we were your age. It was the great Harry Blackstone, Sr. We got to meet the magician backstage. We told him we wanted to be magicians just like him. He gave us our first magic set. Actually he didn't just hand it to us; he caused it to float over to us. I know how he did it now and its fun, but back then it really freaked us out. I want to pass this special gift he gave me and your grandfather on to you—please take care of it."

Alex opened the box carefully and saw the most wonderful things. A set of shiny copper cups with small dark green knit balls, several red sponges shaped like rabbits, a red and a blue deck of cards, an old black wooden wand with a hollow white tip, five tarnished brass coins, and some beautiful silks of all different colors.

"Remember, son, there are rules of magic. Magic Rule Number Two: keep the secret a secret unless you are teaching it to other magicians. If you tell your audience how a trick is done, unless you are teaching magic, the mystery vanishes—and the fun disappears.

If someone insists on knowing how an illusion is performed, do what my friend Brad Barton does. He asks them if they really want to know. If they say "yes," he says 'You'll really be disappointed.' If they insist, he pauses, then dramatically says, 'I do it... I do it very well, thank you!' Then he says, 'I told you you'd be disappointed!'

Magic Rule Number Three: Do a trick only once for your audience. The first time you perform the effect they will be fooled, but the second time they will know what to expect and be more likely to figure it out.

Magic Rule Number Four and Five: Practice, practice.

Magic Rule Number Six…

"Practice!" Alex interrupted gleefully. Then he stopped, confused, "But you left out rule number one. What is Rule Number One?"

"Good catch, son. Rule One is the most important rule of all. Rule One—*Have fun!* If you are having fun, your audience will too. The magic will be more magical and mysterious and people will want more.

You might have noticed that there are not a lot of professional magicians out there. It's because people give up; but if you practice and put the time into the trick, you can master what seems to be impossible and if you make it fun, you will practice."

"Thank you so much! I promise I will practice all the time!" Alex said excitedly.

"Good. I'll see if I can talk your grandfather into having you come by the theater after school. I need a hand with all my props and it will give you a chance to learn the profession of magic."

"I'll help you talk him into that," Alex said, looking at his grandfather and mouthing the word "please" over and over again.

"Well, it's time for us to get going. Thanks for the show, Raven. We will see you soon." Grandpa shook Thomas' hand and Alex thanked him again. They started to head up the stairs.

"Alex." Alex turned around.

"You know, if you're going to be a magician, you should have a magic name—we call that a "stage name." Your grandfather had a name, The Amazing Ambrose. How about calling you the Amazing Alexander in honor of your Grandfather?"

"What do you think, Alex?" Alex's grandfather asked, obviously hoping Alex would agree.

"I think it is perfect." Alex grinned, "Thanks!"

While his grandfather drove home, Alex eagerly looked through the old magic set Raven had given him.

"So your name was The Amazing Ambrose, huh Grandpa?"

"Yes, it had a nice ring to it back in the day."

"So, Amazing Ambrose, what are the little red sponge rabbits for?" Alex asked.

"They are called 'sponge bunnies' and you will learn soon enough what they are for, oh Amazing Alexander!"

Notes

Many professional magicians like Harry Blackstone Sr. and the Great Harry Houdini kept journals and letters of their performances and the different patter that helped them make their magic more fun, mystifying and even educational. If you want to be a great magician, you too should keep track of changes you make in your patter, what things went right or wrong in a trick, and what things you can do to make an illusion better. Refer often to your notes, keep improving, and someday your too may become a legend like Blackstone or Houdini—or Alex!

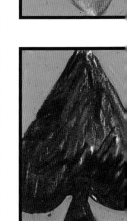

Million Dollar Bill Trick

Effect:
The magician produces two one dollar bills. The bills are then folded. When they are unfolded again they have changed into a one million dollar bill.

Props:
Two one dollar bills and a million dollar bill. You can purchase a million dollar bill at a magic shop or online at www.TheAmazingAlexander.com. If you do not want to use a million dollar bill, you may use a five, ten or twenty dollar bill. All of the bills must be crisp and of the same quality. Good props are critical to good magic. Keep them in good condition. Prepare both bills by folding them into eighths as described below – each fold exact and neat. First fold the million dollar bill exactly as shown then fold the other two the same way. Fold them individually so they will be exactly the same.

Constructing the Illusion:
Unfold the million dollar bill. Apply rubber cement or double-sided tape to the back of one of the folded one dollar bills and attach it to the lower right edge of the million dollar bill, lining up the edges exactly as show in the illustration. I use rubber cement. It sticks securely yet, when the bills get worn, you can rub the cement off and spend the bills (well, not the million). Make sure to ask Mom or Dad to help you glue the bills.

This is the patter that Alex uses as he performs the Million Dollar Bill Trick. Notice the steps to the illusion as they correspond to the patter.
(Step 1) Yesterday I reached into my pocket and I only had two dollars.
(Step 2) I wished I had more money, but I only had two one dollar bills.
(Steps 3-7) I started to put the two dollar bills back into my pocket…
(Steps 8-9) …but then I noticed that I no longer had two one dollar bills. I had a one million dollar bill! I was very surprised and had to check both sides to make sure it was real. It was real! I was so happy and wanted to make sure my money was safe, so I folded the million dollar bill up and started to put back into my pocket. Suddenly I saw that it wasn't a million dollar bill anymore. It had turned back into two ordinary one dollar bills. I must have been dreaming!

Performing the Illusion: (Diagrams are from the Magician's view – away from the audience.)
Practice performing the "show" (steps 1-6), as Alex did, in front of a mirror until your motions are smooth and effortless.

1 Remove folded gimmicked bills from your pocket and hold them with both hands (the million dollar bill always facing you).

3 …sliding your finger upward.

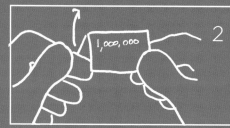

2 Open dollar bills by placing left forefinger into front fold of the bills and…

4 Partly unfold the dollar bills with your left fingers as shown, while holding the folded (hidden) million dollar bill between your right thumb and three fingers.

5 Finish unfolding the dollar bills with your left fingers, keeping the million dollar bill hidden from your audience's view. They now see the front of the unfolded dollar bills.

7 Refold the dollar bills again so they are now folded in half then half again (horizontally) with a fourth of a one dollar bill still showing.

6

Still holding the right lower corner of the bills and the hidden folded million dollar bill, rotate the bills horizontally clockwise, placing the million dollar bill into the fingers of your left hand. George Washington is now facing you. Your left fingers now completely cover the million dollar bill.

Let go of the right side of the bills. Reach in front of your left hand with your right hand, keeping the fingers of your right hand together. With the right hand blocking the view of the million dollar bill contact the edge of the million dollar bill with your right thumb. Push the bill into your right hand with your left thumb. (The bill swivels horizontally clockwise on your thumbs.) You can just turn the bills with your left hand and place the bills in your right hand under the cover of your right fingers, but the swivel movement also works nicely.

You have now completed the "show". Practice this in the mirror until it is smooth. Show it to your mom, dad, brothers and sisters and your dentist. If they say, "So what? It's two one dollar bills," you have done an excellent job of hiding the million dollar bill.

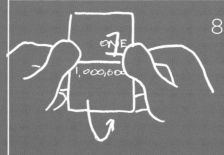

8 Using your middle fingers, fold the bottom half (the million dollar bill) forward and upward so an eighth of the million dollar bill is showing. (You can enhance the illusion by blowing a puff of breath on the bills as you fold the million dollar bill into view.)

9 Now unfold the million dollar bill the same way you unfolded the ones (steps 2-5) this time, keep the one dollar bills hidden and show only the million dollar bill.

Now show both sides of the million dollar bill and then transform it back into two one dollar bills by following the steps exactly as you did before when you transformed the one dollar bills into the million dollar bill.

You could end the trick at the beginning of this step and put the million dollar bill in your pocket. You could also transform the million dollar bill back into the ones as indicated at the end of this step. Some magicians prefer to change the million dollar bill back into ones since one dollar bills are so common and spectators tend not to ask to examine or get a closer look at a dollar bill.

There is another good reason to change the million dollar bill back into two ones. You can have two one dollar bills identically folded in your pocket without the attached million dollar bill in case your audience insists on examining the bills.

Justin S. Meitz

He performed his first illusion at the age of 3 and was buried alive at the age of 6 (fortunately for his parents the sand box was only 3 feet deep). The Mysterious Magical Meitz was born in a small town of 500 people. It used to be bigger, but people kept disappearing! Justin Meitz was reading books before he could stand and writing books before he could walk. They were colorful stories that drew pictures that never quite stayed in the lines.

On an ordinary day, you might find Justin reading the mysteries of Sherlock Holmes to his students, and teaching them magic, to open their minds to all kinds of possibilities – or you might find him locked in a box by his young apprentices and quite unable to get out.

Whether locked up or not Justin is right now working on his next great trick that The Amazing Alexander will learn. Are you ready to learn it too?

Thank you…

…God. Without You this book would not exist – in fact nothing would exist.

…Megan, for being my beautiful supportive wife and critiquing my writing – but not me.

…family. For believing in me – even when I am locked in a box and can't get out – and you wonderful students for giving me terrific story ideas (and occasionally locking me in that box).

…and especially, Tom Cantrell [Raven], for being my creative editor and friend and helping me say what I want to say just the way I want to say it.

Matthew C. Jones

Matt started drawing when he was two years old. His father, a professional artist, built for him a miniature drawing table that he put next to his own. For years they sat next to each other, father and son, big artist and little artist, drawing and painting. Matt would not have been able to illustrate this book without the guidance of his father, the inspiration of his mother and loving family, and his supportive sweetheart, Taylor.